Potatoes at Turtle Rock

This
PJ BOOK
belongs to

_____

_____

JEWISH BEDTIME STORIES and SONGS

For Ubi and Richie and Leo
—S.S. and A.S.F

For Rich —A.S.M.

KAR-BEN PUBLISHING, INC.
A division of Lerner Publishing Group, Inc.
241 First Avenue North
Minneapolis, MN 55401 USA
1-800-4-KARBEN

Website address: www.karben.com

Library of Congress Cataloging-in-Publication Data

Names: Schnur, Susan, author. | Schnur-Fishman, Anna, author. | Steele-Morgan, Alexandra, illustrator.
Title: Potatoes at turtle rock / by Susan Schnur and Anna Schnur-Fishman ; illustrated by Alex Steele-Morgan.
Description: Minneapolis : Kar-Ben Publishing, [2016] | Summary: "Annie leads her family on a nighttime journey around their farm to celebrate the first night of Hanukkah. At each stop along the way Annie uses riddles (and potatoes) to mark old traditions and start new ones"—Provided by publisher.
Identifiers: LCCN 2015040960 (print) | LCCN 2016004619 (ebook) | ISBN 9781467793216 (lb : alk. paper) | ISBN 9781467793230 (pb : alk. paper) | ISBN 9781467793247 (eb pdf)
Subjects: | CYAC: Hanukkah—Fiction. | Riddles—Fiction.
Classification: LCC PZ7.S36442 Po 2016 (print) | LCC PZ7.S36442 (ebook) | DDC [E]—dc23

LC record available at http://lccn.loc.gov/2015040960

Manufactured in China
1-38323-20138-4/12/2016
111625K1/BB0916/A6

Potatoes at Turtle Rock

Susan Schnur and Anna Schnur-Fishman
illustrated by Alex Steele-Morgan

KAR-BEN
PUBLISHING

"Hey, can Ubi come?" Lincoln shouts as we pass our goat on our way to the woods.

"It's up to you, Annie," says Mom. "You're in charge tonight."

"Then why stop with Ubi?" I say. I lift the henhouse door and tuck Richie inside Mom's jacket.

"No eating the Hanukkah candles," Lincoln warns Ubi.

"*Mehhh,*" says Ubi.

Our family has its own traditions
when it comes to Jewish holidays. On Hanukkah,
if it's snowing, we celebrate in the woods. And tonight it's
really snowing! Dad carries the lantern high and Ubi leads
the way. I pull along a sled with a box of secret packages.

"I've planned four stops," I say when we get to the woods. "Old Log. Squeezy Cave. Billy Goat's Bridge. And we'll end at Turtle Rock."

"A viable plan!" Dad says. (Dad likes big words.)

When we get to fat Old Log, we sit down. Ubi tries to sit on Lincoln's lap, but Lincoln pushes him off.

I open the box and lift out my first secret package. "Here's a riddle. When Great-Grandpop was a little boy in his *shtetl*, the winters were really cold and the walk every day to his *cheder* was really long," I explain. "How do you think his mom kept him warm?"

"Ooo, I know!" Mom shouts. "She put a chicken in his coat!"

"She made him hop to school inside a giant sleeping bag?" Dad suggests.

"She let him skip school on really cold days!" guesses Lincoln.

"Nope," I say. I open the package and toss two still-hot potatoes to Dad, two to Lincoln, and two to Mom. I put two in my own two pockets. "She put hot potatoes in his pockets! Try it!"

Ubi *mehhs* hopefully.

"Sorry, Ubi," Lincoln says. "Goats don't have pockets."

"Mmmm, steamy," says Dad.

We put the lantern in the snow and dance around Old
Log, singing a Hanukkah song, and making funny shadows.
Finally I yell, "On to Squeezy Cave!"

Once we're all huddled into Squeezy Cave, I ask Lincoln to blow out the lantern.

"It's spooky in here," Mom says. "Richie just hid his head under my arm."

I want to hide my head under Mom's arm, too. *Why did I plan such a scary stop?* I think.

"Hey, Ubi!" I say (pretending he's the one who's scared).
"You can cuddle up with me." I can't see him in the pitch black,
but I can smell his terrible breath as he plops down on me.

"Okay, everybody. Here's the second riddle. Why is it so dark?"

"Because we're in a cave in the middle of the night?" Dad guesses.

"Is it because Hanukkah comes at the darkest time of the year?" asks Lincoln.

"Right," I say. "The days are the shortest, the nights are the longest, and there's almost no moon the whole week. But on one night there's never any moon at all. Which night?"

Ubi *mehhs*.

"Ubi says tonight," Dad translates.

"Correct!" I say. "Look outside. On the sixth night of Hanukkah there is never a moon!"

"Cool," says Lincoln.

"Let's each name some things that really scare us," I say.
"Creaky noises in the kitchen at night," says Mom.
"Snakes," says Lincoln. (He is *very* afraid of snakes!)
"The federal deficit," says Dad
"Uncle Ron's latkes," Mom says.
"Ms. Finklestein, my teacher's aide," I sigh.
Richie peeks his head out and squawks.

"Don't worry, Richie," I say. "The dark *is* scary. That's why we light Hanukkah candles. Next stop, Billy Goat's Bridge!"

Dad re-lights the lantern, and Lincoln holds it high as he leads the way.

At Billy Goat's Bridge, I say, "Everyone take one potato out of your pocket, and let's line them up on the bridge."

I lift out another secret package. "Here's the third riddle: What do we use for a menorah when we're out in the woods?"

Everybody looks puzzled.

Out of the package I take – CANDLES!
I make several holes in the potatoes—nine altogether—
and then I put six candles and the *shammash* into the holes.
"A potato menorah!" says Dad. "Annie, you're ingenious."

We light the candles, say the blessings, and sing *"Al Ha'Nissim."* It's beautiful with the snow and dark all around us and the candles lighting up Turtle Rock Creek.

We sit quietly until the very last candle sputters out.
Even Richie looks thoughtful.
"That was amazing," says Lincoln. "I love Hanukkah in the snow."
"Thank you, Ubi, for not eating the menorah," Mom says.

We all just want to stay here, but eventually I announce, "Last stop, Turtle Rock!"

When we get to Turtle Rock, it's super icy, but Mom pulls us to the top. Lincoln has pushed Ubi up from behind.

I open up my last secret package.

"And now for a Hanukkah treat! Everybody, take out your last potato," I say. I set four plates out in the snow, along with a salt shaker, a stick of butter, maple syrup, and four big spoons.

"Yum!" says Lincoln. "Baked potatoes and snow cones!"

We eat hot potatoes dipped in butter and salt, and a freezing spoonful of fresh snow that we drizzle with syrup.

"Potatoes sure are versatile tonight," says Dad.

"To Hanukkah!" I announce, giving Ubi half my buttered potato. He snorts a thank you.

"You have been a very good chicken," Mom tells Richie, giving him a bite of potato.

Lincoln and I make dreidels in the snow.

Then Mom makes up a little prayer:
We give thanks for celebrating in the peaceful woods
on the darkest night of the year.
For the lantern and candles and magical snow.
For the beautiful sounds of the creek.
For safety and warmth, for Great-Grandpop's mom,
for Ubi, for Richie, for each other.
We give thanks for the blessings of Hanukkah!
Together we shout, "AMEN!"

The Story of Hanukkah*

The story of Hanukkah happened a long, long time ago in the land of Israel. At that time, the Holy Temple in Jerusalem was the most special place for the Jewish people. The Temple contained many beautiful objects, including a tall, golden menorah. Unlike menorahs of today, this one had seven (rather than nine) branches and was lit not by candles or light bulbs, but by oil. Every evening, oil would be poured into the cups that sat on top of the menorah. The Temple would glow with shimmering light.

At the time of the Hanukkah story, a cruel king named Antiochus ruled over the land of Israel. "I don't like the Jewish people," declared Antiochus. "They are so different from me. I don't celebrate Shabbat or read from the Torah, so why should they?" Antiochus ordered the Jewish people to stop being Jewish and to pray to Greek gods. "No more going to the Temple, no more celebrating Shabbat, and no more Torah!" shouted Antiochus. He sent his guards to ransack the Temple. They brought mud and garbage into the Temple. They broke furniture, tore curtains, and smashed the jars of oil that were used to light the menorah.

This made the Jews very angry. One Jew named Judah Maccabee cried out, "We must stop Antiochus! We must think of ways to make him leave the land of Israel." At first, Judah's followers, called the Maccabees, were afraid. "Judah," they said, "Antiochus has so many soldiers and they carry such big weapons. He even uses elephants to fight his battles. How can we Jews, who don't have weapons, fight against him?" Judah replied, "If we think very hard and plan very carefully, we will be able to defeat him." It took a long time, but at last the Maccabees chased Antiochus and his men out of Israel.

As soon as Antiochus and his soldiers were gone, the Jewish people hurried to Jerusalem to clean their Temple. What a mess! The beautiful menorah was gone, and the floor was covered with trash, broken furniture, and jagged pieces from the shattered jars of oil. The Maccabees built a new menorah. At first they worried that they would not be able to light their new menorah, but they searched and searched, until at last they found one tiny jar of oil—enough to light the menorah for just one evening. The Maccabees knew that it would be at least eight days until they could prepare more oil, but they lit the menorah anyway. To their surprise, this little jar of oil burned for eight days. The Jewish people could not believe their good fortune. First, their small army had chased away Antiochus' large army, and now the tiny jar of oil had lasted for eight whole days!

The Jewish people prayed and thanked God for these miracles. Every year during Hanukkah, Jews light menorahs for eight days to remember the miracles that happened long ago.

* The transliterated word *Hanukkah* can be spelled in a number of different ways – including *Chanukah, Chanuka,* etc.